# CIRCLE
# OF LOVE

By Monique Gray Smith    Illustrated by Nicole Neidhardt

Heartdrum
An Imprint of HarperCollinsPublishers

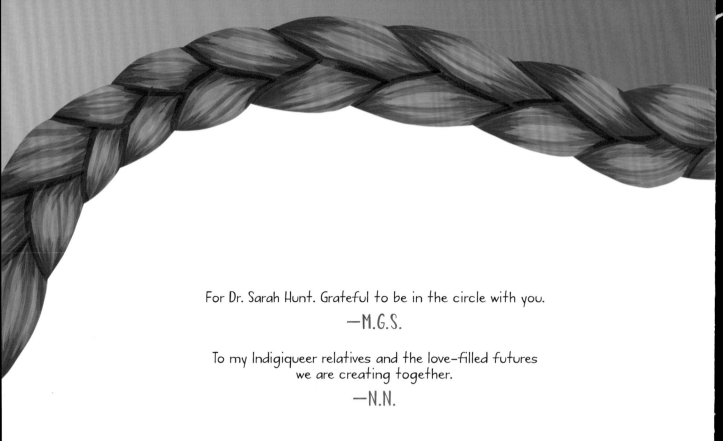

For Dr. Sarah Hunt. Grateful to be in the circle with you.
—M.G.S.

To my Indigiqueer relatives and the love-filled futures
we are creating together.
—N.N.

Heartdrum is an imprint of HarperCollins Publishers.

Circle of Love

Text copyright © 2024 by Monique Gray Smith

Illustrations copyright © 2024 by Nicole Neidhardt

ISBN 978-0-06-307870-3

The artist used an iPad Pro to create the digital illustrations for this book.

Typography by Caitlin E. D. Stamper

23 24 25 26 27 RTLO 10 9 8 7 6 5 4 3 2 1

First Edition

# FOREWORD

We welcome someone into our home or space in nêhiyawêwin by saying "tawâw."
The beauty of this word is that it means so much more than a simple welcome.
On a deeper level, it means "there is always room." In many ways, this is what Molly
is sharing with us in this story as she introduces us to the people she loves. She
reminds us that there is always room in our hearts and in the circles of our lives.
The circle is a place of equality and equity and, ultimately, love.

Tonight, we are gathering at the intertribal community center for a feast.
When my friends and Elders greet us, I feel joyful.
When Kôhkom and her wife, Kôhkom Raven, sing a welcome song,
I feel connected.

LOVE IS LOVE

When my teacher says, "Tânisi, Molly," I feel important.

When I read books to the babies, I feel kind.

When my uncles and I play peekaboo with their baby, I feel love.

# LOVE IS LOVE

When I draw pictures with my friend Sophie,

I feel creative.

When my sibling plays their music, I feel energized.

When they teach us jingle dance steps, I feel motivated.

LOVE IS LOVE

When my cousins take us outside to the playground, I feel excited.
When the wind blows in my hair and the sun warms my face,
I feel powerful.

When I see Sarah and Karolina tend the community garden,
I feel appreciative.

LOVE IS LOVE

When I smell the sweetgrass burning, I feel peace.
When I watch my parents prepare for ceremony,
I feel respect.

When I help make the food offering, I feel honored.

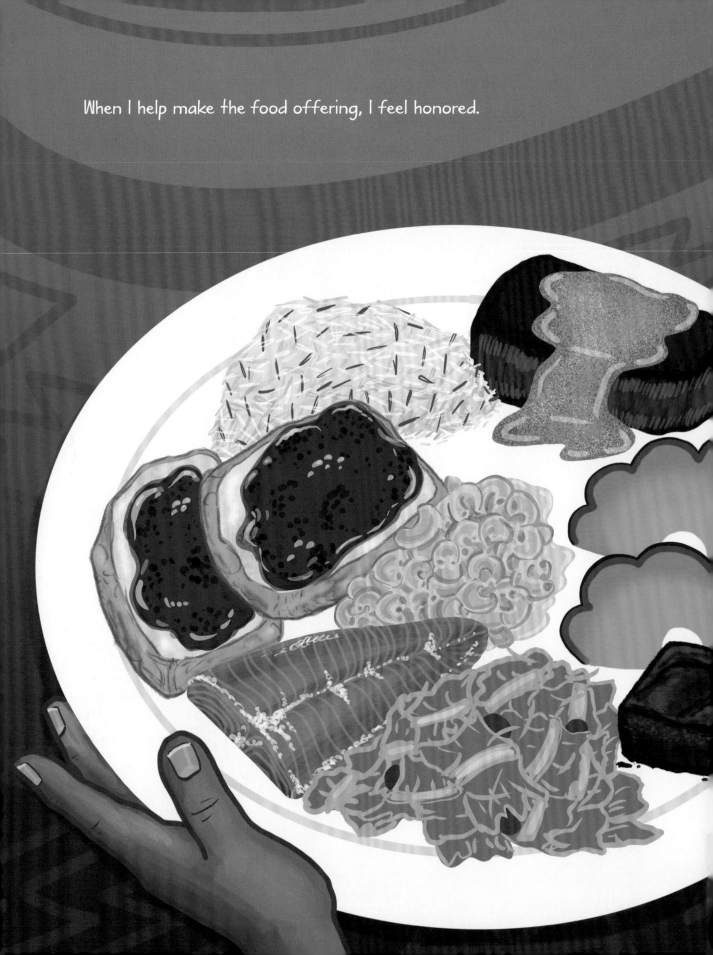

When a prayer is said to bless the food, I feel thankful.

When I eat my soup and bannock, I feel nourished.

When my friend Billy and his moms sing
to give thanks for dinner, I feel happy.

LOVE IS LOVE

When my auntie speaks to me in nêhiyawêwin, I feel proud.

When I sip my medicine tea, I feel the warmth swirl down my throat.

When I watch Joshua bead, I feel awe.

# LOVE IS LOVE

When I curl up under Kôhkom Raven's arm, I feel safe.
When I close my eyes, I can see the stories that are being told.

When my family and community come together, I feel love.

LOVE IS LOVE

# AUTHOR'S NOTE

Writing this book took me, a two-spirit person, back to my childhood. It was a time when I didn't understand what was going on inside me and didn't have anyone I could talk to about my feelings. There were no role models in my family, and I never saw myself reflected in any books or TV shows. I wanted Molly to have a different experience. *Circle of Love* is what I would have loved my childhood to have been like and what I hope it is like today for children and young people who identify as LGBTQIA2S+.

The idea for this book initially came from the Northwest Portland Area Indian Health Board, which was looking for a way to share the two-spirit teaching with children. I revere those initial visionaries who wanted a book for young people so that children could see their family members in a story. I am grateful to Morgan Thomas and Alessandra Angelino for their shepherding of this project from the very beginning. Much gratitude to the Elders, Marlon Fixico and Sadé Heart of the Hawk Ali, who helped guide the initial discussions and concept exploration.

# COMMUNITY CENTERS

In this story, we join Molly for a feast at an intertribal community center. She introduces us to those who make up her family and community, and we experience her love for each of them.

Sometimes, stories about acceptance or inclusion imply that there has been a decision to love. What Molly shares with us is what is truly at the heart of family and community: love and respect for one another. Woven into community is the teaching that everyone has a place in the circle. Having a place in the circle also means we have responsibilities: to be kind and respectful, to share our gifts and help out when we can.

One of the greatest gifts Indigenous urban settings provide is a sense of community. Whether that is through people participating in programs or attending community gatherings, ceremonies, feasts, or educational activities, these centers provide a healthy, vibrant place to belong.

Non-Native federal, state, provincial, and territorial legislation and policies have shaped the demographics of Indigenous people in urban communities across what is currently called North America. The United States' Indian Removal Act of 1830 and Canada's Indian Act (initially written in 1876) included policies of forced removal from tribal homelands, often causing relocation to urban areas.

First Nations and Native leaders realized the need for cultural gathering spaces—resulting in intertribal centers in cities such as Baltimore, Chicago, Dallas, Minneapolis, Phoenix, and Seattle in the US and more than 110 urban friendship centers in Canada. Their community-tailored programming includes job training, childcare, Elder and youth activities, employment assistance, counseling, and family support initiatives.

# CULTURE

You will notice in the story that there are patterns of four and that cultural nuances are woven throughout the story. In each example, centered on Molly's emotions, a specific cultural practice is highlighted. These range from singing a welcome song to preparing for ceremony to speaking nêhiyawêwin to learning new jingle dance steps to saying a prayer to bless the food.

You will also note in the flow of the book that each stanza has three examples of love, with the last one always being LGBTQIA2S+ and then the repetitive line "Love is love." I wrote it with this rhythm for a couple of reasons: 1) the reader hears two examples of love and then the LGBTQIA2S+ example of love and, following that, the consistent message "Love is love"; 2) to honor the importance and sacredness of the number four in my teachings.

When you think about why the number four is meaningful, there are four seasons, four traditional medicines—cedar, sage, sweetgrass, and tobacco—four directions, and four valves that control the flow of blood in and out of the heart.

## LGBTQIA2S+ | Lesbian, gay, bisexual, transgender, queer, intersex, asexual, two-spirit, plus

As Molly introduces readers to members of her family and community who are LGBTQIA2S+, we begin to appreciate her love for each of them. These are important people in her life, and she loves them all. As she shares her feelings with the reader, we are reminded that love is love.

"Two-spirit" is a relatively new term and honors the role of nonbinary gender people in precontact and contemporary Indigenous Nations. Two-spirit identity can include special roles in community/society and ceremony and may be seen to have sacred status. Two-spirit people are often the ones who care for others and may be healers or caretakers.

The term was introduced at the LGBT Native American gathering in 1990 by Elder Myra Laramee and is a translation of the Anishinaabemowin term "niizh manidoowag," two-spirits.

Two-spirit can have a variety of meanings. It can include a person who identifies as having both a masculine and feminine spirit and those who identify as nonbinary, gay, lesbian, bisexual, transsexual, transgender, and/or queer. Two-spirit people can have other intersecting identities, such as being a Black Native person or one whose first language is Spanish.

Within all aspects of Indigenous cultures, there are both similarities and differences between each Nation. This is also true for how Nations both historically and in modern day honor and respect those who identify as two-spirit and the gifts they have been blessed with.

# ACTIVITY

This activity has been designed to foster social and emotional awareness among a group of children, as well as to support children in calming their nervous systems and paying attention to their breathing. To start, have the children sit in a circle and go around the circle, having each child share one word that describes how they are feeling. You can use a variety of feeling charts or other tools to support children so they use a vocabulary beyond happy, sad, mad. Those are also valid responses, but part of this activity is to expand children's vocabulary and understanding of feelings and words that they might associate with what they are feeling inside. You can lead by demonstrating, "I'm feeling _____."

Encourage them to use "I'm feeling" again as a tool to continue developing social and emotional intelligence. Always give the children the option to pass. We may not know what is going on in a child's life or how their temperament may influence sharing in a class setting. The option to pass ensures their dignity is upheld.

After they have shared, thank each child. This is supportive of their social growth, as everyone experiences their own value in being heard, as well as the importance of listening to each other in the circle.

Being in the circle also ensures that each child can be seen and heard and that no one has a more important or less important role. Once the circle is complete, then share a breathing activity with the children. Have them slowly breathe in for a count of four, hold breath for four, release air to a count of four, and hold again for four. Have them do this four times and then ask them how they feel.

TÂNISI, MOLLY!

# GLOSSARY

**kôhkom (KOH-kum):** The official translation is "your grandmother"; however, it is most often used by grandchildren when they address their grandma. *Kôhkom* is increasingly accepted as an English word and thus can follow English rules for capitalization.

**nêhiyawêwin (nay-hee-YAH-way-win):** Cree language

**tânisi (TAHN-sih):** Hello. How's it going?

**tawâw (tuh-WOW):** Welcome. Come in. There is always room.

# A NOTE FROM CYNTHIA LEITICH SMITH, AUTHOR-CURATOR OF HEARTDRUM

Dear Reader,

You are so, so loved! You are a dearly loved member of our human family. You are loved by your ancestors. Maybe you have an animal relative—like a dog or cat or fish or hamster—who loves you, too. Love is a feeling. In this book, Molly experiences many wonderful feelings while spending time with her family and community. Her story is about joy, respect, connection, and, most of all, love.

This picture book is published by Heartdrum, a Native-focused imprint of HarperCollins Children's Books, which publishes stories about young Native heroes by Native and First Nations authors and illustrators. I feel happy that we are publishing this book because of its heartfelt poetic language, because of how the art brings Molly's feelings to life, because it highlights urban intertribal centers, and because it celebrates diversity within Indigenous families.

Mvto,
Cynthia Leitich Smith

In 2014, We Need Diverse Books (WNDB) began as a simple hashtag on Twitter. The social media campaign soon grew into a 501(c)(3) nonprofit with a team that spans the globe. WNDB is supported by a network of writers, illustrators, agents, editors, teachers, librarians, and book lovers, all united under the same goal—to create a world where every child can see themselves in the pages of a book. You can learn more about WNDB programs at www.diversebooks.org.